FOR ELO, VIKTOR AND GUSTAV.

This is a second edition. First published in English in 2018 by Flying Eye Books,
an imprint of Nobrow Ltd. 27 Westgate Street, London E8 3RL.

Carls flyglexikon © Carl Johanson, 2017, first published by Rabén & Sjögren, Sweden, in 2017.
Published in agreement with Rabén & Sjögren Agency.

Text and illustrations © Carl Johanson 2018.

Carl Johanson has asserted his right under the Copyright, Designs and Patents Act, 1988,
to be identified as the Author and Illustrator of this Work.

Published in the US by Nobrow (US) Inc.

Printed in Poland on FSC® certified paper.

ISBN: 978-1-911171-65-2

Order from www.flyingeyebooks.com

ALL KINDS OF

PLANES

A BOOK BY
CARL JOHANSON

FLYING EYE BOOKS

LONDON I NEW YORK

ANGULAR PLANE

TWO-PART PLANE

CAKE PLANE

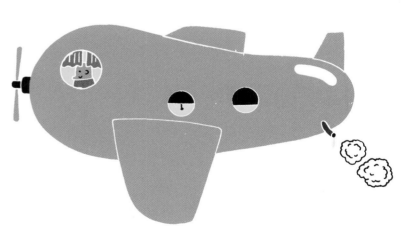

COSY PLANE

CRASHED PLANE

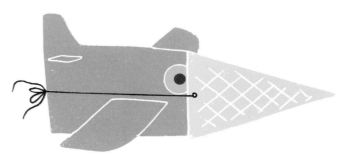

SHY PLANE

ROCKET STOOL

WOODEN PLANE

POO PARACHUTE

APPLE PLANE

ABSTRACT ROCKET

LAZY PLANE

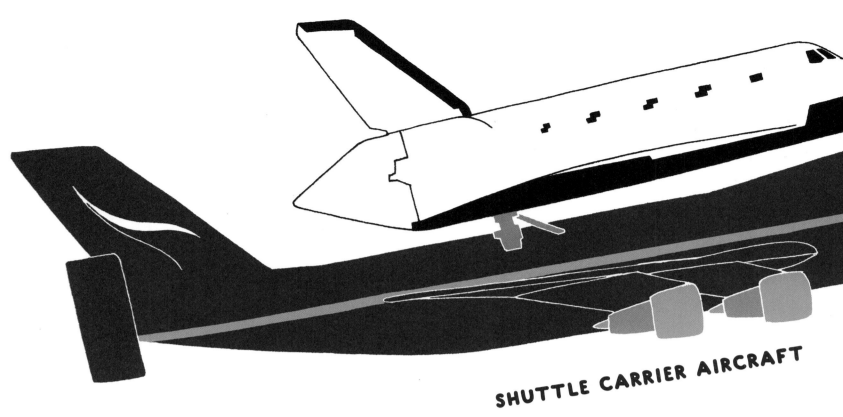

SHUTTLE CARRIER AIRCRAFT

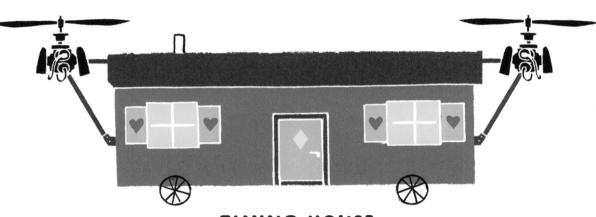

FLYING HOUSE

CARGO AIRCRAFT

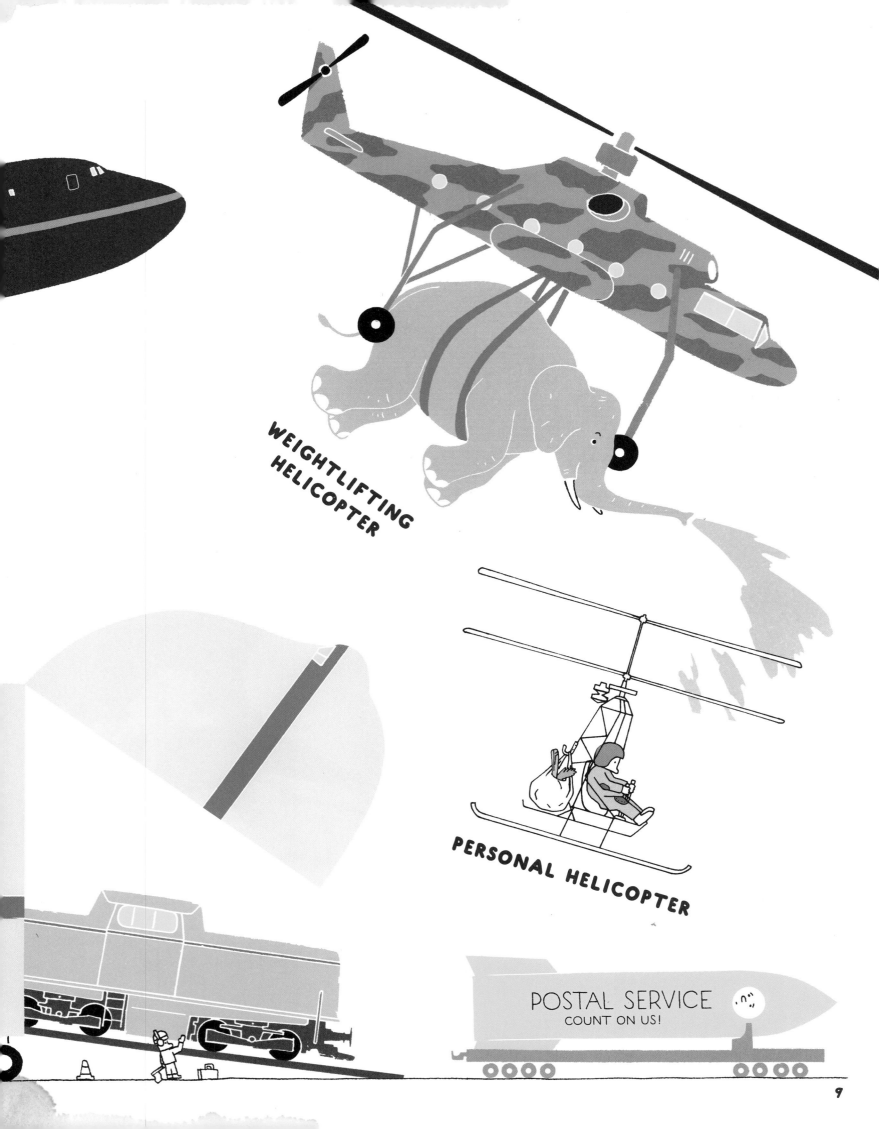

WEIGHTLIFTING HELICOPTER

PERSONAL HELICOPTER

POSTAL SERVICE
COUNT ON US!

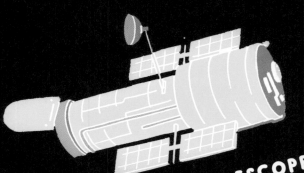
HUBBLE SPACE TELESCOPE

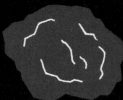
ASTEROID

METEOROIDS

SATELLITE

ROCKET

SPACE SHUTTLE

METEOR

INTERNATIONAL
SPACE STATION

ASTRONAUT

LAIKA

SPACE DEBRIS

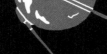

SPUTNIK 1

LUNAR LANDER

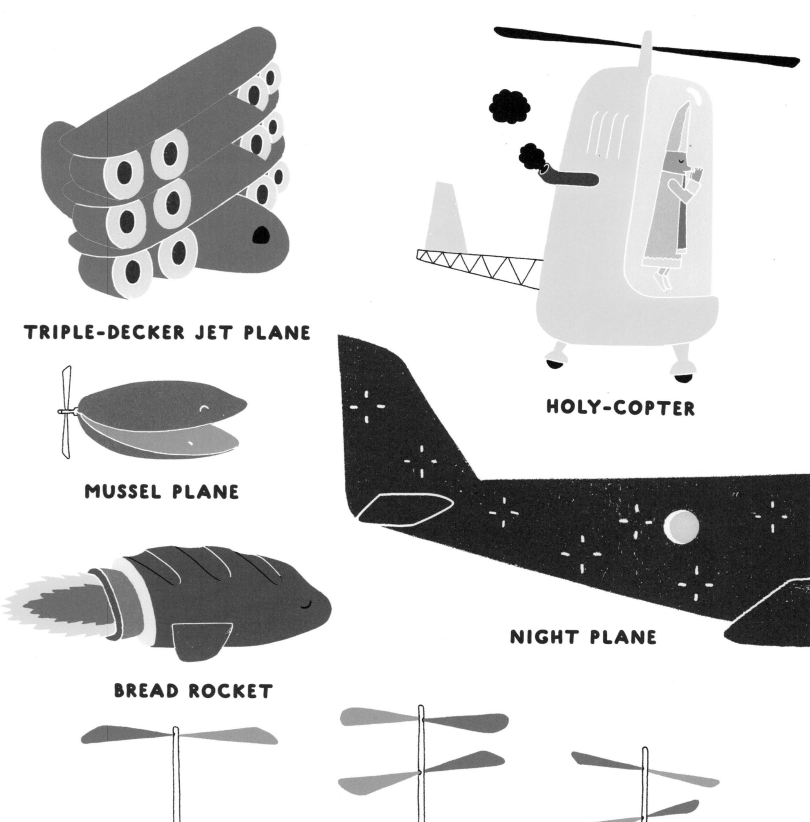

TRIPLE-DECKER JET PLANE

MUSSEL PLANE

BREAD ROCKET

HOLY-COPTER

NIGHT PLANE

FRAGILE TRANSPORT

LIGHTWEIGHT PLANE

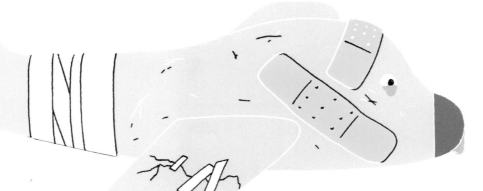

INJURED PLANE

MAKESHIFT PARACHUTE

DECONSTRUCTED PLANE

STONE PLANE

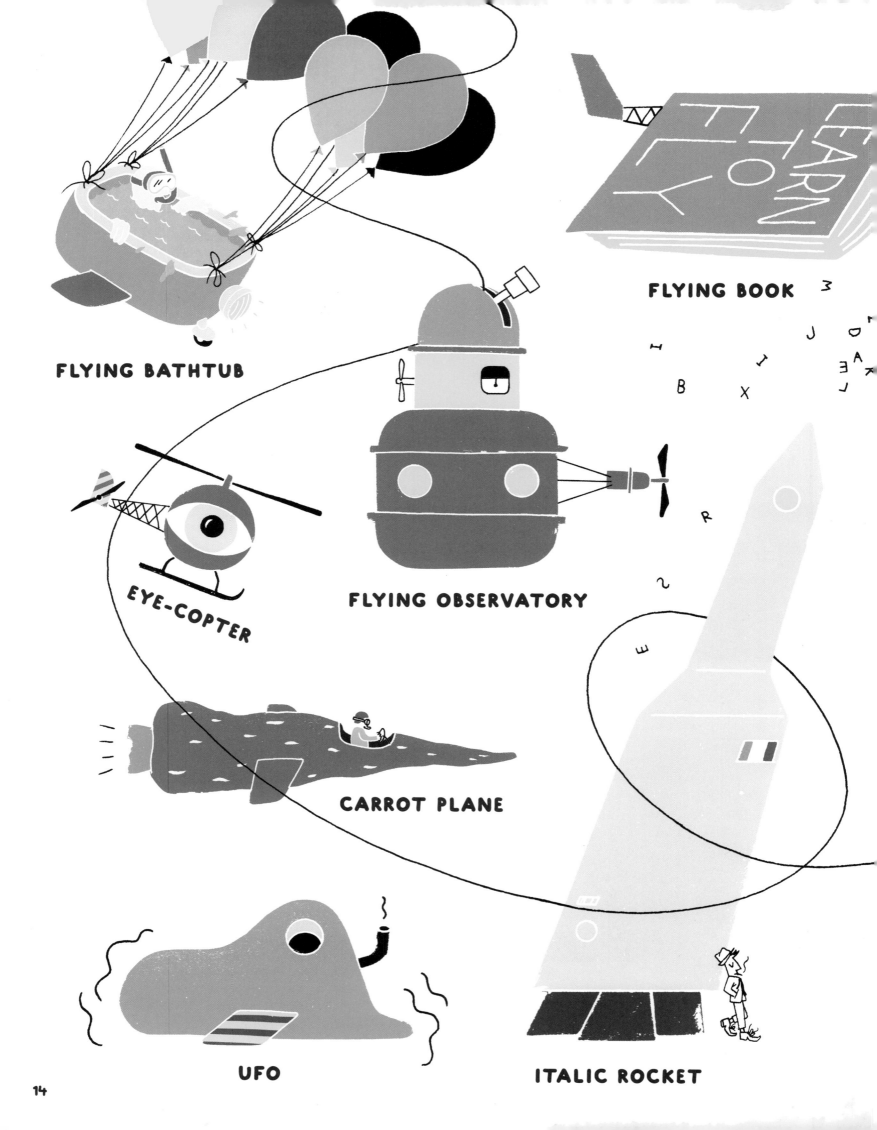

FLYING BATHTUB

FLYING BOOK

EYE-COPTER

FLYING OBSERVATORY

CARROT PLANE

UFO

ITALIC ROCKET

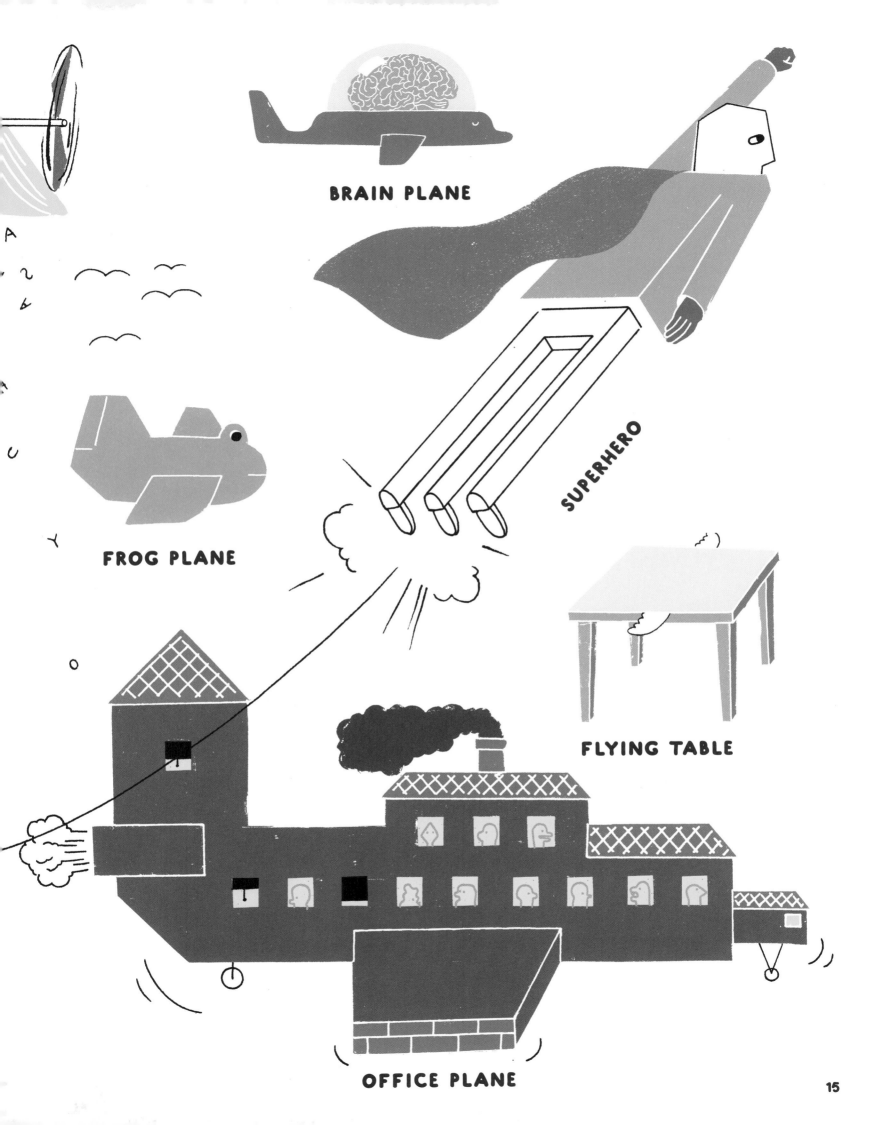

BRAIN PLANE

SUPERHERO

FROG PLANE

FLYING TABLE

OFFICE PLANE

DRONE

VERTICAL AIRCRAFT

EXPERIMENTAL AIRCRAFT

AMPHIBIOUS HELICOPTER

EJECTOR SEAT

'FLYING BANANA' HELICOPTER

RADAR DOME PLANE

RESCUE HELICOPTER

FIGHTER JET

AVION III

BLÉRIOT VIII

MONTGOLFIER
HOT AIR BALLOON

BLÉRIOT VI

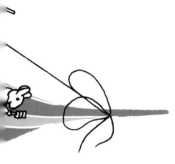

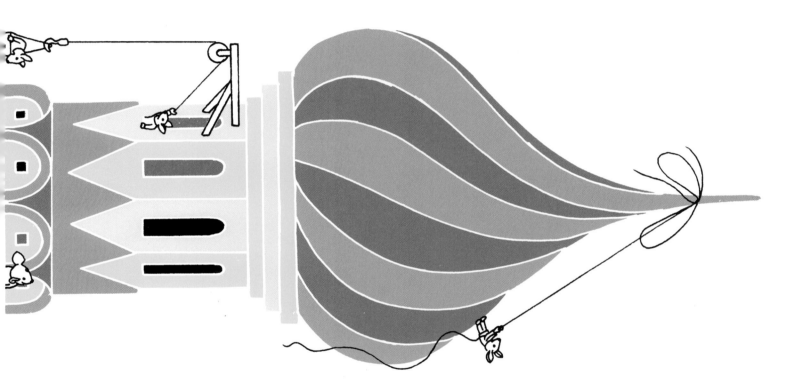

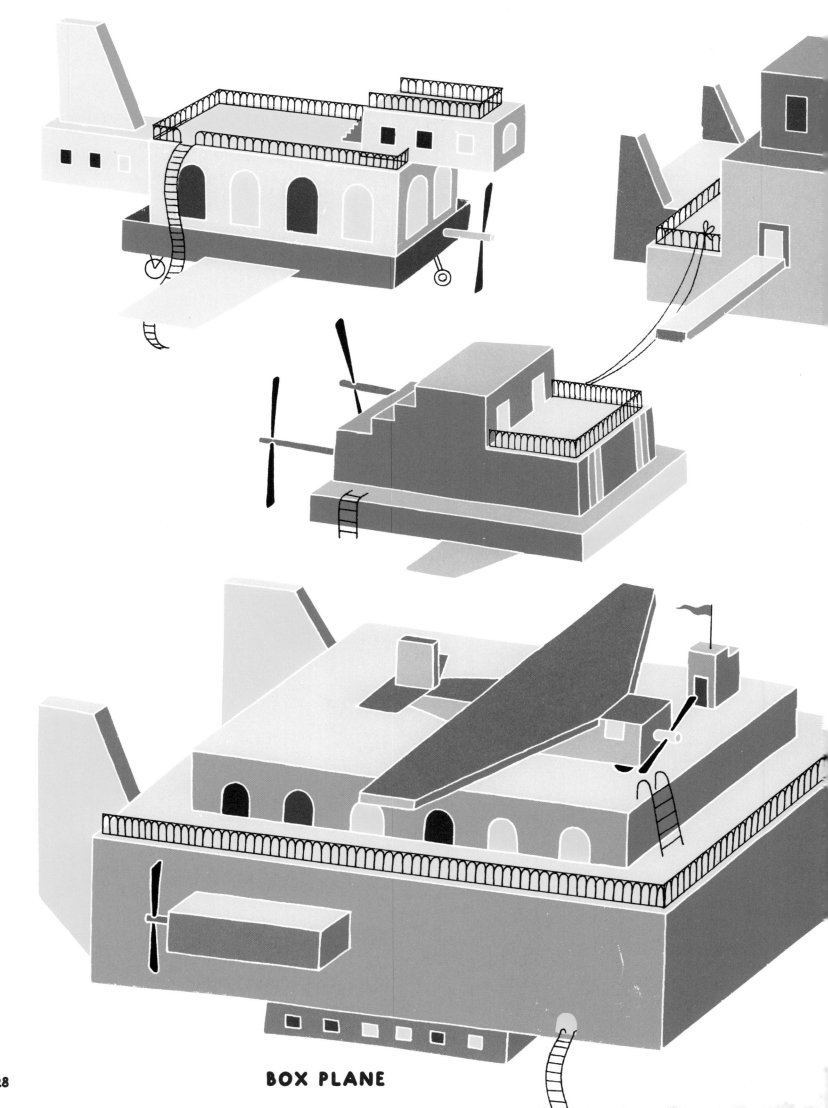

BOX PLANE

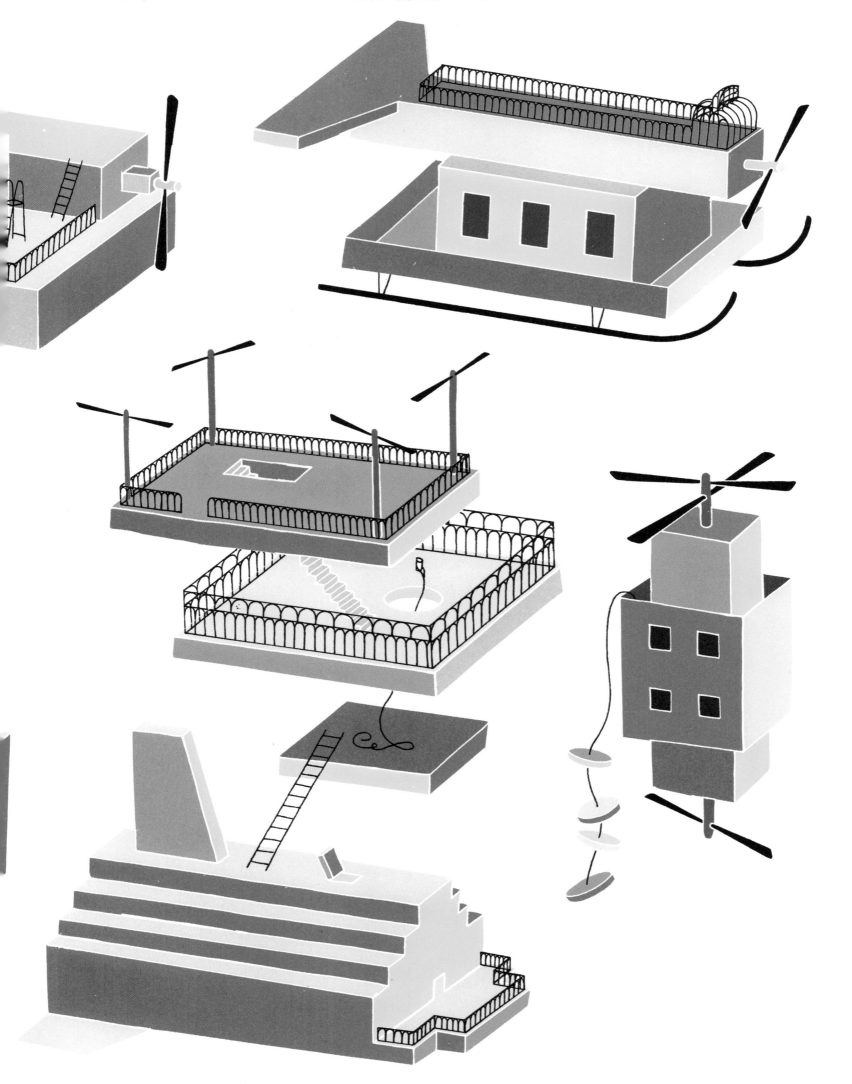

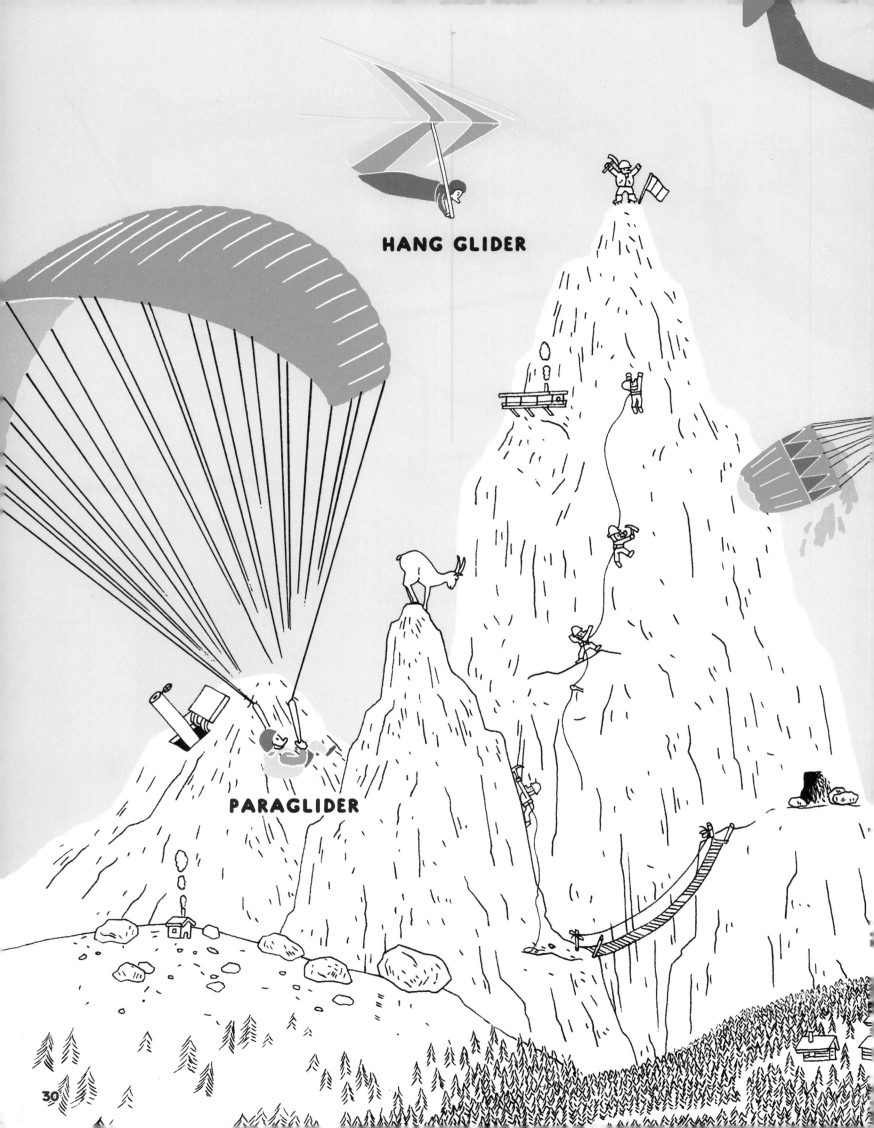

HANG GLIDER

PARAGLIDER

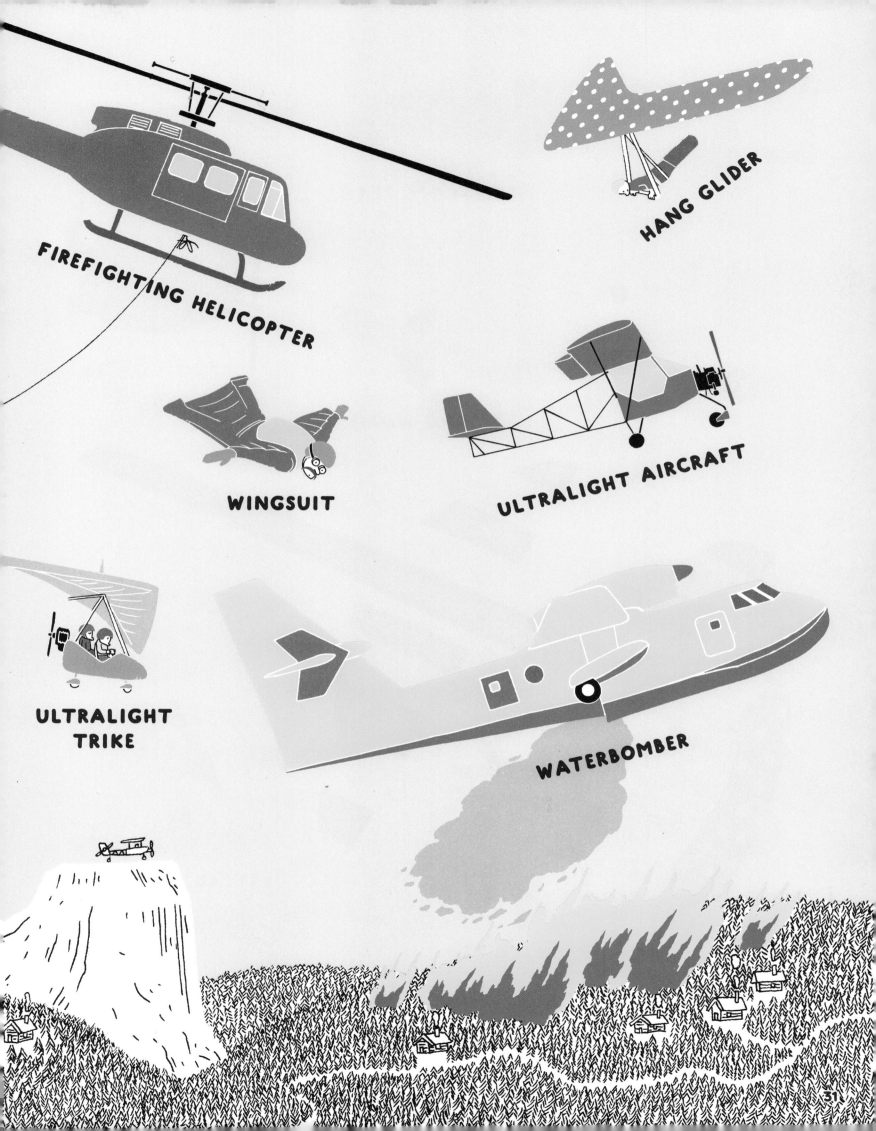

FIREFIGHTING HELICOPTER

HANG GLIDER

WINGSUIT

ULTRALIGHT AIRCRAFT

ULTRALIGHT TRIKE

WATERBOMBER

TELESCOPE PLANE

BABY PLANE

FLYING WORM

POO-COPTER

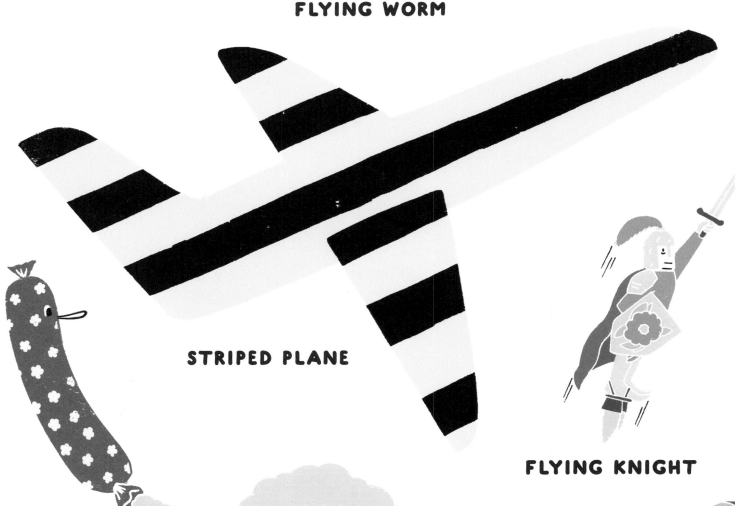

STRIPED PLANE

SAUSAGE ROCKET

FLYING KNIGHT

SIMPLE ROCKET

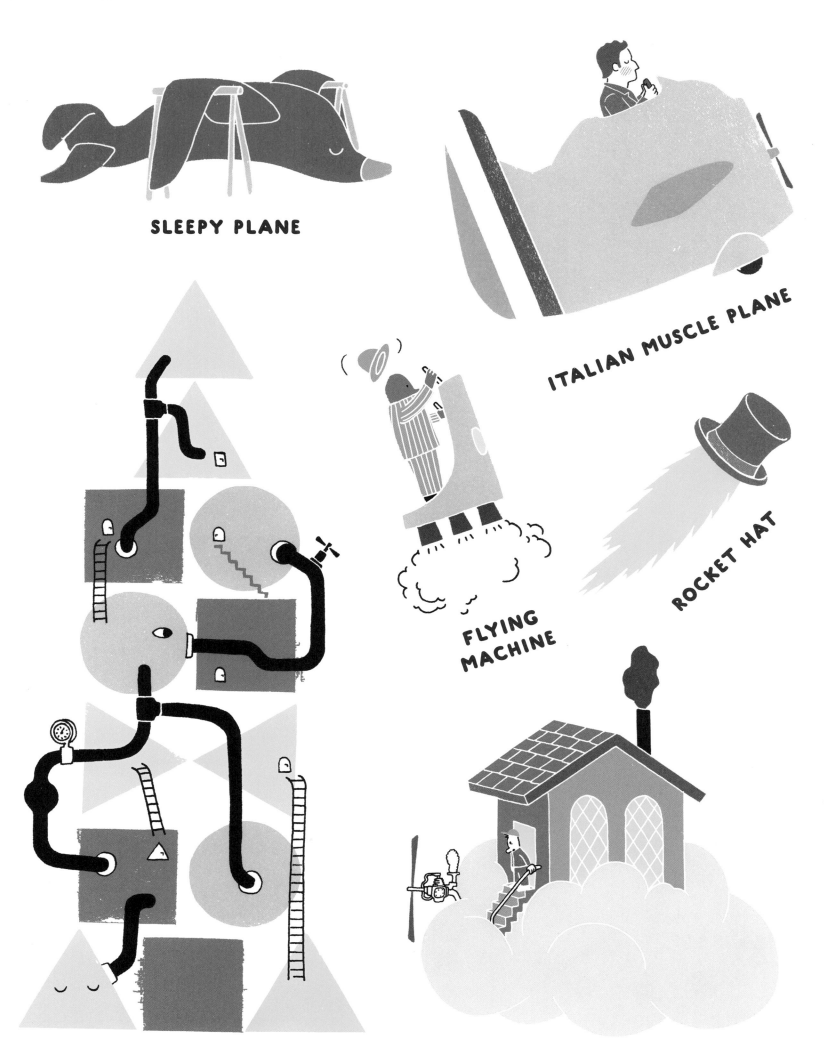

SLEEPY PLANE

ITALIAN MUSCLE PLANE

ROCKET HAT

FLYING MACHINE

BAUHAUS ROCKET

FLYING STUDIO

FLYING MAGNET

FLYING ARK

FLYING HAT

36

HOT AIR BALLOON PARTY

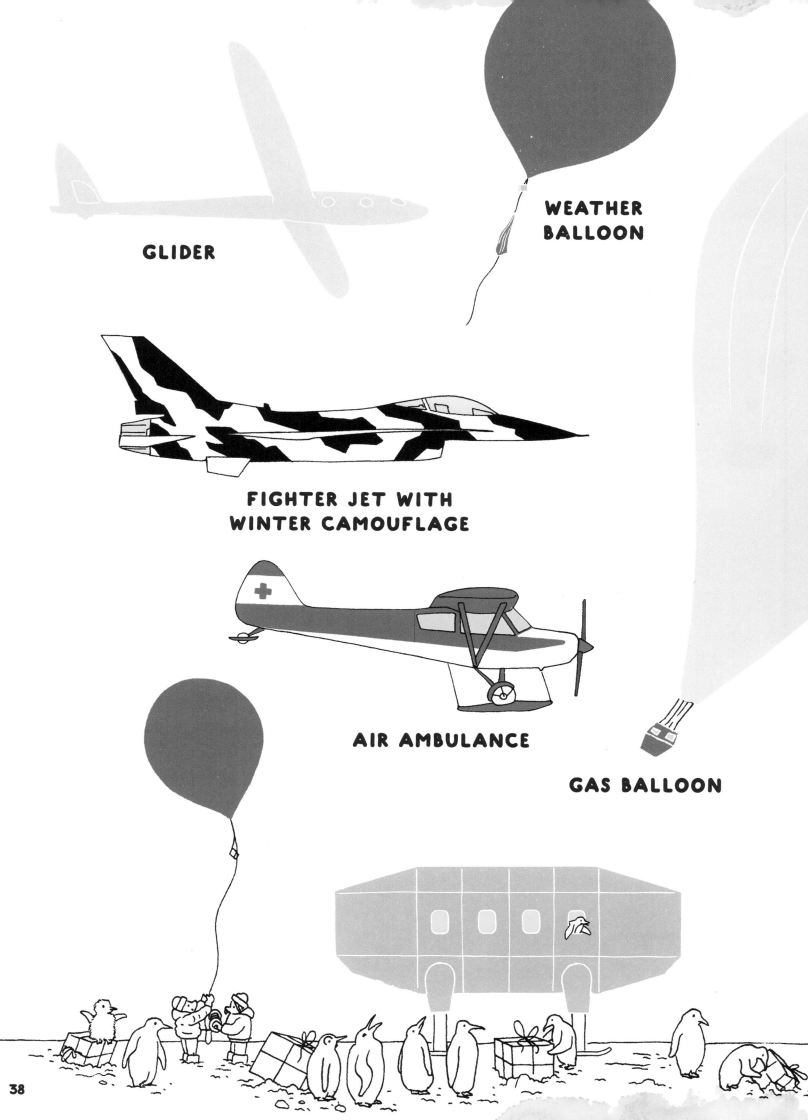

GLIDER

WEATHER
BALLOON

FIGHTER JET WITH
WINTER CAMOUFLAGE

AIR AMBULANCE

GAS BALLOON

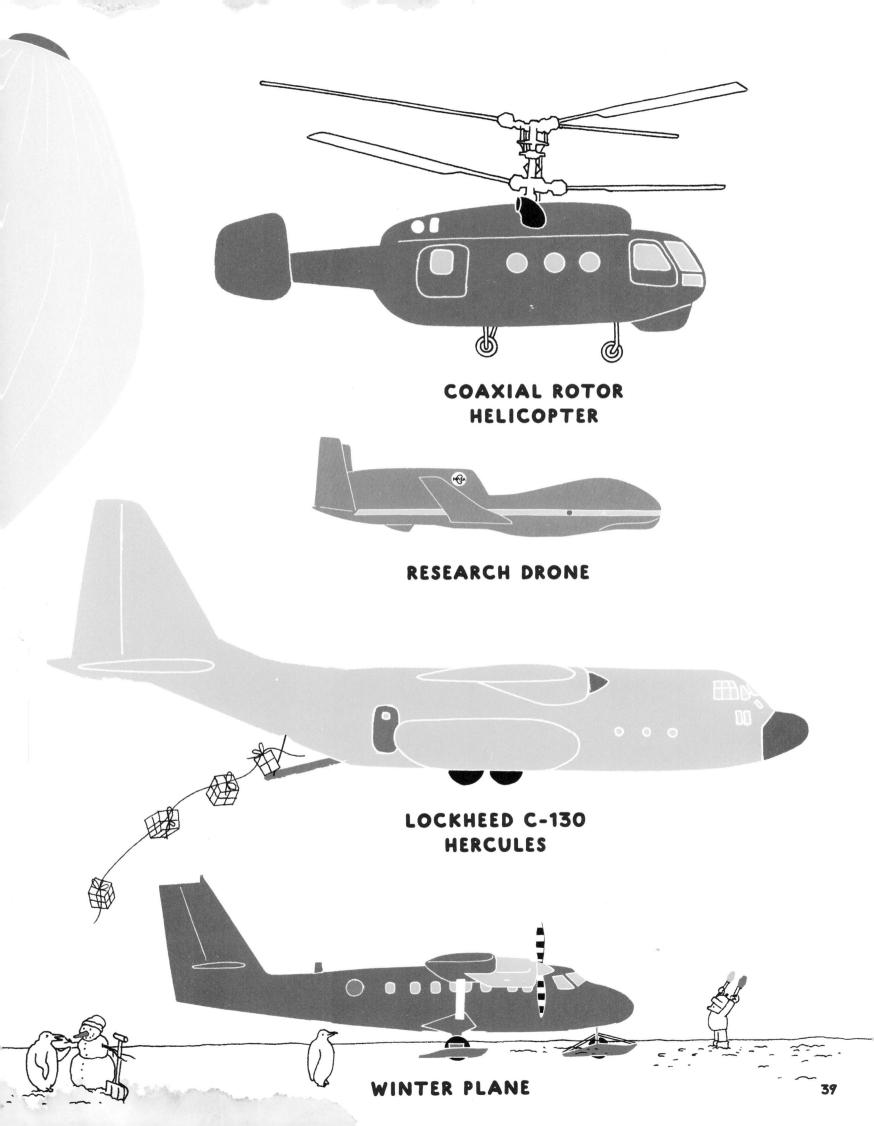

**COAXIAL ROTOR
HELICOPTER**

RESEARCH DRONE

**LOCKHEED C-130
HERCULES**

WINTER PLANE

INDEX

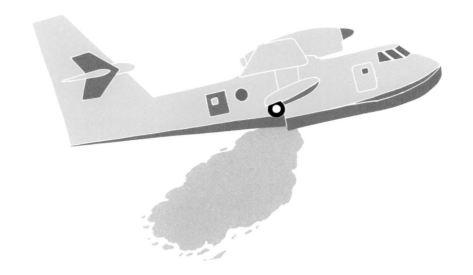